PRAISE FOR SHELTA'S SONGBOOK

"Enter a world where myth and mortality tango at the crossroads of choice and chance... a slice of what it means to have a timeless human experience. It's a gift that reminds the rest of us mortals that we're not broken, and that even in our solitude we are not alone."

— Beth W. Patterson, Author and Musician

"Every page will have you in awe. Talon captures emotion with vibrant detail."

— Elysia Lumen Strife, Author of the Infinite Spark Series

"An intriguing prelude to a world of magic and mystery that's sure to captivate anyone with a dreamer's spirit."

— Kat Turner, Author of Hex, Love, and Rock & Roll

"Shelta's thoughts laid bare. A compelling introduction to the universe of the *World Tree Chronicles.*"

— Avery Ames, Author of Cambiare

"*Shelta's Songbook* wraps story around song, and song around story, in intertwining spirals that dance across illustrated pages. If you wish to travel between worlds, this book will take you there."

— Alexander Forbes, Author and Professor

LEIA TALON

SHELTA'S SONGBOOK

POETRY AND PROSE FROM THE VAULTS OF THE KEEPER OF LOST SOULS AND STORIES

THE WORLD TREE CHRONICLES

Copyright © 2020 by Leia Talon. All rights reserved.
Thank you for buying an authorized edition of this book.
Please respect copyright laws by not reproducing or distributing this book by any means without permission, other than excerpts in credited mentions, which are appreciated.
The publisher encourages reviews.

This is a work of fiction. Names, characters, places, and incidents are a product of the author's imagination. Locales and public names are sometimes used for atmospheric purposes. Any resemblance to actual people, living or dead, or to businesses, companies, events, institutions, or locales is entirely coincidental.

Published by Rhiannon Publishing, 2020
British Columbia, Canada

www.LeiaTalon.com

Cover Design by Alexandra Purtan ~ Fenix Book Cover Designs
Main Illustrations by Glazkova Irina ~ Nutriaaa / depositphotos.com
Tree illustration title page by Kevron2002 / depositphotos.com
Dragon illustration page 92 by Rorius / depositphotos.com
Book Layout by Rhiannon Publishing

Shelta's Songbook / Leia Talon ~ First Edition
ISBN: 978-0-9879923-3-8

Sometimes the riskiest roads are the ones that lead us home.

Shelta

TABLE OF CONTENTS

FROM THE KEEPER

I HAVE WATCHED SHELTA since the beginning, when she was born through the World Tree into a future far from the time and place she was conceived.

I am not the only immortal who watches her. She's our greatest hope, even if we don't agree on imagined outcomes. It is forbidden for gods to interfere in the realm of humans. We do anyway, of course. The subtlest of interactions ripple into unknown consequences.

The unpredictable nature of Shelta's travels through time and reality would've broken some, but it has only made her music more exquisite, her spirit more complex in its beauty. Shelta has endured loss after loss—friends and lovers held for but a blink of time, and so many songbooks left behind.

With this collection, I have captured stray threads. Treasures that would have otherwise been lost. Shelta's art feeds my immortal soul, setting me aflame.

Although most of Shelta's writing is poetry, I've discovered a few short stories tucked between sketches and notes. I've gathered lyrics scrawled on scraps of paper, unwillingly abandoned. Occasionally, I reach through the World Tree and transcribe a song as Shelta sings it.

Magic is a recurring theme in her work, as is love. And loss. When I read these, I wonder if some part of her soul knows from whence she came.

And I wonder what she will do when she finds out...

THE DANGEROUS ONES

Bring me your secrets. Ask me to dance.
Give me your heart in a glance.
Show me your soul in fleeting words,
I'll ride the blood-ocean surge.

I am reflected in the eyes of those
Who cut through the layers, dare to get close
Enough to touch the essence unseen:
Inside me lives a goddess-queen.

I've always found home with the dangerous ones,
Like my soul needs an edge to dance on.
Reach into the truth of it all
And listen to the call… Listen to the call.

THIS PATH

This path beckons,
Loam soft beneath,
Until a misplaced step
Turns up sharp.

Brambles taunt,
Fae shapes dancing in
Light and leaves.
Laughter on the wind.

Roots make way
For feet to leave the
World behind.
The path snakes on.
It twists and rambles,
Heedless of fog,
Flirting with disaster
And possibility.

This heart
Knows how to fly,
And how to shatter.
This body knows how
To tumble,
And how to dance.

Sometimes the trail forks,
And the previous way
Is lost forever.
Sometimes it leads
To adventures unknown.
To seas of uncertainty,
And freedom.

TOO FAR FROM THE SEA

I want to dive off this cliff, become one with the water
But I'm too far from the sea.
There's no going back, the path's disappeared
And I've got too much to carry.

One foot then the other, keep marching along.
How far have I gone? Will I ever get there?
Got to stay strong, I pay my way in songs,
But I've only ever had a taste.

I'm a fool, I'm a fiend, I'm stuck in between
The pull and push of need.
Like the tide closing in, drowning within,
I'll go wherever it leads.

I'm alive, I'm alive, I'm barely surviving,
And thriving all the same.
I'm afraid of the dive, of the looming goodbyes,
But I want to play the game.

I keep on and on, hope I haven't gone wrong,
They say heed your heart and be free.
I'd jump but I can't, you won't be there to catch me,
I'm too far from the sea.

I'd surrender to you, to the current of truth,
And all that it would mean.
But fate tortures me, it's all out of reach,
I'm too far from the sea.

THE CANVAS OF MY MIND

I close my eyes,
I leap, I fly.
Hold tight to my sword,
And lash out.

Worlds within worlds,
Layered within,
Spiraling into
Forever.

How many lifetimes
Rush through my soul,
Demanding their songs
To be sung?

I may look still.
Quiet. Pensive.
But I am a thousand
Screams unfolding.

Flowers blooming,
Petals bleeding,
Painting themselves
Upon the canvas
Of my mind.

THE KEY TO MY SOUL

I am an unsolvable riddle.

I've combed through countless libraries,
Questioned wisdom keepers,
And sought answers in the stars.
I have turned pages until the song
Of paper slicing through air
Became a lonely soundtrack
To the mystery of my life.

The answers I seek
Remain out of reach.

The vault that contains me is vast.
I reside in its depths,
Swallowed by shadows.
Its walls are transparent.
I can touch the world around me,
But not belong.
I can taste the promise of love,
But never keep it.

I'm trapped.
Locked into a game I don't understand,
With rules that only apply to me.
Uprooted, again and again,
My search for understanding
Is a litany of failure.

The barest hints of clarity
Brush my skin like delicate wings,
Sparkling gold in the corners of my eyes.

THE DRUM OF THE GODDESS

My heart beats to the drum of the goddess,
Soul blazing with the fire of a star,
But the dream glitters, fading,
Dancing out of reach.

This body yearns to find new horizons,
Swim in enchanted springs and
Shiver beneath a lover's touch.
But time's whims steal every chance.

Life finds a way; bending in the wind,
Hiding from thought-storms
In stories and daydreams,
Plotting escape with each page turned.

Fiction bleeds into reality.
The goddess beats her drum.
I raise my foot, step toward her.
Into the illusion,

Where endless fjords,
Time-traveling dragons,
And god-blooded lovers
Are not so out of reach.

I'M NOT BROKEN

I am not broken,
Though sometimes it seems that way.
Grief and acceptance visit in turns.

I invite them in,
Let them tell their stories.
If I'm willing to listen, perhaps I will learn.

What do we have in the end,
But our stories?
Our dreams, our dares, our darkest nights…

My scars don't ruin me,
They make me stronger,
And add to the art I create with my life.

RIPTIDE

Life reaches out, and takes me under.
Can't move, can't shout.
I don't know where I'm going.
I'm blinded by a symphony
So deafening I can't breathe.
Flying through everything that exists
As it streams through me.

Like a riptide.
It pulls me like a riptide.

Sacrifice holds a bitter freedom.
Loss shoves me off a familiar peak.
I'll reinvent my life, again.
Always alone in the end.
I've got no roots. I've got no roots.

Like a riptide.
It pulls me like a riptide.

Lures me like moonlight.
Squeezes my throat tight.
Blinds me like sunlight.
Sucks me through time.

Like a riptide.
It pulls me like a riptide.

ECHO

Echo, echo, my lover.
Together at last under these stars.
The sky moves slowly as we
Discover ourselves through each other's hearts.

So many possibilities.
You invoke bewilderment.
Your words are like letters I wrote to myself
And time seems to have thinned and bent.

Echo, echo, my mirror.
Closest of spirt kin ye be.
We journey along in this scented forest
Bare feet, bared souls, minds free.

Deep, deep, deep run your roots.
Dark eyes sweet and knowing.
Your touch makes me shiver and sigh,
Strong and tender like water flowing.

And I believe I know exactly how to
Fall in love in a day and a night.
Softening into your warmth
My world feels right.

Surely the universe is up to something,
Laughter like ripples of light.
I play in this body because the dance is exquisite
And your reflection of me is beautifully bright.

GIVE ME MORE

I'm a fiend. All I want is more.
Epic beats in my pounding heart.
Thirst without hope of satisfaction,
Hunger splits me apart.

Music like hands on my skin,
Mouth open to draw breath.
Give me more. Please, I need it.
Got to live to defy death.

Waves of passion rise and peak,
Tension twining through me.
Muse like sunlight in my blood,
Blinded by fantasy.

Crooned words promise paradise,
But it's nothing of the sort.
It will break, shatter, self-destruct.
This song is always too short.

I'll be left starving again,
Wicked laughter echoing from afar.
Build me up. Tear me down.
Burn me like a shooting star.

THE BRINK OF NIGHT

Between the dark and light
Time's heartbeat stops.
Peace spreads her wings
Beside the talons of doom.

Their unlikely courtship
Weaves chaos and order,
Companions in the unfolding
Of existence.

This is the space between the breath,
The place where exhale turns to inhale.
A reckless dive into the unknown,
A risk taken for fate unshown.

Time's rhythm grows.
Life rests, but does not sleep.
As balance spins its pirouette,
Valour emerges from the deep.

SEEKING THE ROOT

I strip myself of pretense,
Despite the trepidation.
Layers of false protection
Fall like clothing to the floor.

My ego thinks me special,
But I am no better or worse
Than anyone else
On this human adventure.

The ten-thousand-rules
Are but veils,
Shadows and shimmerings
Of confusion and control.

How much skin must
I peel away
Before I find the root
Of insecurity?

I am afraid to shine,
Yet I must.
My soul demands it,
Drags me to the light.

The instinct to hide,
My secrets, myself,
Is so deep that I
Cannot touch the bottom.

Naked, I shiver
Beneath my own gaze.

RAIN

Rain washes the air.
Cleans ash off leaves.
Quenches the earth.
Deepens all the greens.

Breathe.
Cozy up.
Listen.
Settle in.

Let the cloud-tears
Nourish the land.
Nourish the soul.

Let the heart-sea
Calm in the wake
Of the storm.

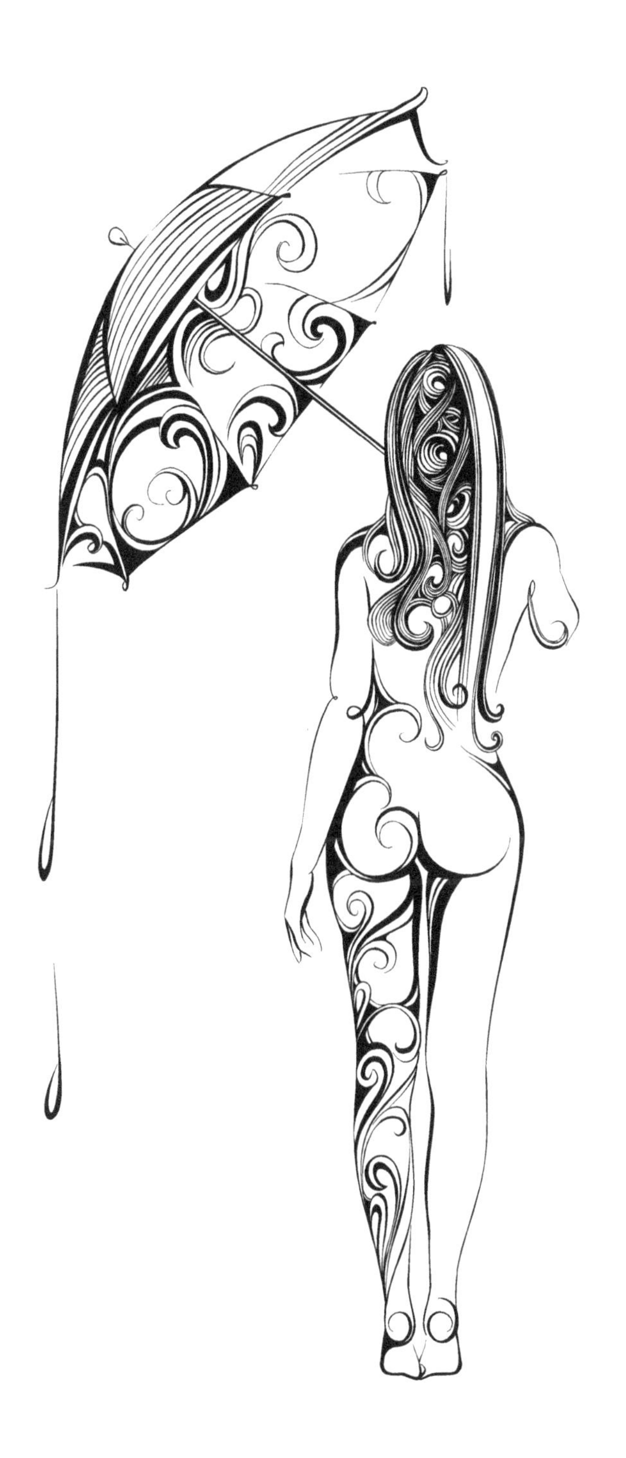

REBORN

Newness in being, I walk.
Hummingbird sings by.
Breeze kisses leaves.
Sky deepens to dusk.

Old thoughts circle:
Twin vines named
Lonely and Longing.
I cut through them.

New faces form.
A fresh adventure grows
In my imagination.
A love affair with my muse.

The mountain hides the sun.
Cool creep the shadows.
I stride toward home,
In gratitude, and grace.

THE MOON LOOKS ON

Echo on the lake, rumble over ice.
The stars shine on, the stars shine on.

Frost on the trees, smoke in the air.
The moon looks on, the moon looks on.

Quiet so deep it pulls you close.
The night breathes in, the night breathes in.

Thoughts so steep there's no escape.
The moon looks on, the moon looks on.

Dance by the fire, offer a song.
The earth she knows, the earth she knows.

Take it to the pyre, offer up a bone.
The moon looks on, the moon looks on.

Chant as we spin, twirl 'round the sky.
The stars shine on, the stars shine on.

The secret is within, the unseen eye.
The moon looks on, the moon looks on.

WHISPERS OF SPRING

Grow your roots down deep, my dear,
Listen to the Earth.
Tap into the limitless
Energy of rebirth.

Breathe a fresh breath in, this day,
Twirl a brand-new jig.
Wish upon the blossoming.
Hands in soil, dig.

Hear the songs returning now,
Robin's trill, owl's hoot.
Sun coaxes plants to grow,
Nature's humble loot.

Water brings its myriad music,
Wind sings with trees.
Let yourself awaken now,
Set yourself free.

A BREATH OF TIME

I missed you by a breath of time.
Wish you'd stayed to hear
These words heavy in my throat,
Eyes stinging with tears.

I want to ask how you feel
When I sing secrets to the sky.
Does it make you want to run?
Does it make you want to fly?

Surge and pull,
There's a sea
Trapped in my chest,
Trying to break free.

How I wish I could
Trust you with my
Dark-bright fantasy.
You'd think me crazy.

I don't want to lose this love
To walls of fear and
Floods of doubt.
But you've already walked out.

GOOD GIRL, BAD GIRL

Head and heart at odds again, story of my life.
Hit the walls of should and can't,
'Course I'm gonna fight.
Sky child in free fall
Struggling 'gainst the bonds
Of obligation, torn by the need to get gone.

Don't conform to expectations,
Lord help me, but I tried.
A rare few get me,
Others make me want to hide.
I can't lie to myself, I've got to let this ride.
Good girl, bad girl, I got both inside.

Sometimes my reflection
Shows me stories of the past.
Other times I see a change,
Floored by a blast of recognition, newness.
Total transformation.
Creativity flows with renewed motivation.

Never stop asking
What do I want to be?
Where do I want to take myself?
What's the next version of me?
Imagination pushes past dogma and walls,
But the cage closes in as reality calls.

Head and heart at odds again, story of my life.
Don't do what you think I should.
Rebel gonna fight
Against thoughts that limit me
And rules that don't apply.
Good girl, bad girl, I got both inside.

I AM ALIVE

I don't know how to do this, but I'm doing my best.
Tripping down this twisted road,
Heart pounding in my chest.
I try to walk with integrity, with honesty,
And balance responsibility
With a need to be wildly free.

I seem to choose the high road, the hard road,
The dark road, the warned-against road.
These places force me to feel,
To be real, to deal with who I am.

There's magic surrounding me, living inside of me,
Along with uncertainty deep as the sea.
Vast as the sky, I spread my soul wide.
Don't know where it ends, but I'll try, I'll dive.

I am alive.

KNOTS IN THE WEAVING

Do not voice the disappointment.
Let the moment pass.
Spend the words somewhere else,
Wasn't the first, won't be the last.

Nothing but expectations
Crushed. Left to bleed.
Scattered on the floor of my heart,
Another thread in the weft I weave.

Soften, bend, let it go.
Braid hopes together,
Not too tight, round like a nest,
Expanding into forever.

This too shall pass, the goddess whispers.
She takes another strand.
Deftly, gently, stardust smiling,
Weaves it with my hand.

The tapestry is knotted, scarred,
Gnarled like a tree.
Tangles of infinite mystery.
A hidden lock. An elusive key.

It grows, this field of knowing,
This living, quilt-like trance.
The more I let the goddess lead,
The easier it is to dance.

THREADS OF INTIMACY

Crushed resistance settles like ash
On sheets we shouldn't share.
Willing conspirators, your words
Wake the lioness in my soul.

My name on lips I daren't kiss.
The rumble of your voice
Makes its home in my chest.
I lean into your touch.

We dance a careful courtship
Through the inky hours before dawn,
Incinerating ourselves in a fire
That stretches through tendrils of time.

Much is denied, but intimacy
Threads itself through you and I,
Weaving heart-binding breaths
Into a secret tapestry with smoking edges.

UNWELCOME GUESTS

I was already on my knees when
Anger and Depression waltzed in,
Arm in arm, like always.
They started wrecking the place
Like rock stars on a binge.

Anxiety cowered in the corner, shaking.

I crawled to the balcony and
Gulped deep breaths,
But the cold air pierced my lungs,
No warmth to be found.

I glanced over the edge,
As I'd done many times before,
But the fall to crushing oblivion
Was only the illusion of escape.
I wouldn't find any answers there.

I tried to evict my unwelcome guests,
But they crashed back in through the window,
And put a hole in the wall.

So I gave Anger a punching bag,
Covered Depression with a cozy blanket,
And served Anxiety some soothing tea.
It didn't satisfy them, but it helped.

I retreated to bed, knowing
They'd be up to their tricks
Again in the morning.

But, somehow, I'd find the strength to survive.

EMPTY

Nothin's gonna fill this empty,
Only thing I can do is give.
String some notes together,
This is the way I live.

Spread myself out into nothing,
Just a speck in space,
Stardust seeking company,
Music gives me grace.

Seek, go seek the essence,
Retreat, go deep inside.
Ain't no one gonna stop the lonely,
Girl, this is a solo ride.

Sing like light shimmering,
On shards of broken hope.
An uneven, jagged mosaic
Obscured in a haze of smoke.

Pour my soul out again,
For the sake of no one but me.
At least I understand myself,
Trekking through the empty.

EVOLUTION

I am constantly running from myself,
Berating myself,
Surprising myself,
Amazing myself.

These cycles churn relentlessly
In a spiral that expands and contracts.
I am not the same person I was
A day ago. A year ago.

Walk on.
Breathe.
Let go the heavy past.
I've carried it too far.

Move on.
Let go the stubborn hurt.
Release the grudges of fear.
Time to level up.

TEMPTATION

Thank you for your smile,
So graceful in your kindness.
I apologize for being so intrigued.

It seems as though the night
Has swallowed me completely.
And I wonder...

Would your kiss make me feel less lonely?
Would your eyes show your truth to me gently?
Would your touch make me shine so brightly?

Or would it fade like a winter sun?

Thank you for your smile,
Your sweet, inviting smile.
I only look away out of temptation.

STEP BACK

Take a step back, girl,
Before you get in too deep.
Take a step back, girl,
Before you're down on your knees.
Take a step in.
Take a step down.
Have a look around.

What do you want, love?
What do you need to be?
All that soulshine,
All that wild and free
Wants to get out.
I gotta get in tune with me.

Stand on your own two feet.
What do you want to believe?
Breathe it in, and breathe it out,
Into the world.

STREAM OF CONSCIOUSNESS

Entangled in twisted trust,
I stumble to reach your voice.
I swim through thickening lust,
Words like velvet, mouth moist.

Shakespeare spills his glass of
Rhapsody across the ceiling.
Poetry slips past the wine on your lips,
Devastatingly appealing.

Conversations swallow hours.
Dizzy laughter lights my eyes.
My defenses lay at your feet,
In glittering shards of abandoned lies.

I trip over my tongue
Pouring thoughts in offering.
Gone, fallen into your song,
Passion in the pondering.

Here you have my window of truth,
Confessions given, careless.
I'll sacrifice myself to taste
Your stream of consciousness.

LUST'S WISDOM

Lust enters me:
A phantom presence in my too-empty mouth,
An absence of body to tangle myself around,
A void of touch within which to drown,
A wanting that eludes, no respite found.

She tempts me:
To take things too far when I should hold back,
Risk everything to fall, to fly too fast.
Weave what I want into who I am.
To break. To feel. To grow whole again.

She reminds me:
To tend to the music that lives in my soul,
Dive into the wanting, embrace the unknown.
Dig until I find a way to fulfill
This fire that drives me, burns to a chill.

She takes me:
To the edge, to the embers, to walk on the coals.
To dance. To run in the foam on the shore
Of an infinite coastline, each wave that comes
Is a pulse. A thrum in the heart-song.

THE DARK WATERS OF THE SOUL

IT WAS MEANT TO BE a solo trip, but she didn't want to be alone. So, she invited him. The mysterious one. The man whose heathen grace made her blood sing.

They found sanctuary in a forest by a river whose cascades created deep, wide pools. Cedar and mist scented the air. A rope swing hung over dark, cold water, beckoning the brave.

He wandered while she set up camp. Tent. Bedding. Journal. Drum. Sacred stones. Perched on a boulder, with the flow of water on all sides, he drew his swords and moved in a practiced dance. Waiting for her.

When she climbed onto his rock, he gave her the blades. Showed her how to hold them. How to move. How to strike. How to breathe and balance.

His touch brought her to life.

They lingered, drawn together in the seclusion of the wood, serenaded by river and birdsong. She came here to be alone, but asked him to stay. Just one night.

The fire snapped and cackled. They traded words of magic and confession. He held her more fully than she'd ever been held, as if he was made to cradle her.

He had the presence of a faerie king, the soul of a poet. It called to her own. She melted, surrendering a part of herself. A flame grew within as the fire's embers glowed.

In the morning, she asked him to go. Perhaps it was a coward's choice, perhaps it was the noble one. It was supposed to be a solo retreat, after all.

One last time, he embraced her. Body and soul. Before he left, he gave her a sword, like a part of him remained behind. Guarding her.

Alone, she sat by the water, swaying to its soothing song. The fish looked up at her from their little lakes. She conjured the courage to dive from a high rock into the shadowy green, but the thrill escaped her.

The forest was a lonely place without him. She'd set out to make peace with being alone, and there was comfort in the silence, in the gentle sway of the trees... But beneath, in the dark waters of her soul, where the sun couldn't reach, sorrow's shadows bled deep.

She'd sent him away for the sake of a lie. Her almost-lover. The mysterious one. The near-stranger who'd held her like he was holding her spirit along with her limbs.

The binding was unraveling, time burning to ashes. The forest didn't fill her like his fire-bright kindness, even if his sword lent her strength.

His memory would haunt her. A cherished crack in the crumbling shell of her heart. The chance was gone, like the embrace that called her restless spirit home.

DETOURS

Excess, excess, you know I feel it,
Feel it from time to time.
Liquid and smoke in my memory,
Memories in my rhyme.
Drunken fingers trip over their strings.
Dark gravel voice slips her dress off as she sings.

I know that the magic's in the moment, so I hold it there.
Then the present takes my imagination, and strips it bare.
But I'm still attached to my stories,
I love to let 'em fly.
So I swirl my reality in the sky.

I can be inspired in any state,
Of mind in any space.
These detours have their place.

Breathe in, breathe out
You know this body likes to play,
Sway with the rhythm
Inside of me, and I can breathe it out.
But I gotta get comfortable with dancing alone.
If I'm gonna grow it's gonna be on my own.
So excess, excess, let's enjoy this time together
While we have it.
Singing my smoky sexy song voice,
Thinking in fragments.
Between these sliding words I take a moment to think
About the impact of my actions, then I blink.

I can be inspired in any state,
Of mind in any space.
These detours have their place.

NIGHT'S MAJESTY

In the wee hours of the morn
Defenses fall away.
Pretense fades into star-specked black
Overcome by Night's majesty.

Truth stretches out
Seduced by a taste of freedom,
Naked in a fleeting sense of safety
That dissolves with the dawn.

The sun burns.
Layers must be retrieved,
Picked up off the floor for
Fear of being seen.

Judging eyes replace the
Serenity of stars.
Responsibility invades.
Night's freedom melts away.

Truth, still naked beneath the façade,
Clings to sparkling memories.
But hope suffocates beneath the demands of the day,
And sleep steals the promise of the night.

THICK-WALLED TENDER HEART

This thick-walled tender heart's got too many cracks.
I try to cage my love but it comes rushing back
Through slices of canyons, ravines in my chest,
It lights me on fire from my feet to my breasts.

The way this rolls through me,
I know you understand,
But to let my walls all the way down,
I don't think I can.

'Cause I've got all the trust issues,
Want me to count 'em off?
I've got self-doubt in spades,
And a mind that won't stop.

I've got emotions that surf every monster swell,
I try to stay calm—sometimes I do it well,
But when I fall apart, Goddess, what a ride.
Let me patch up this wall, keep that mess inside.

This thick-walled tender heart's got too many cracks.
Put some holes in the walls myself trying to get back
To a place where I can trust myself and more.
Sometimes I fly in the sky, sometimes I'm on the floor.

But the lightning that crashes
From my heart through my veins
Makes me want to blast the walls down
Just to hear you say my name,
But then I'd have no shield,
I'd probably go up in flames,
And I'm afraid...

FOLLOW THE LEADER

FOLLOW THE LEADER, bare feet on hot sand, headed for the ocean, we skip across the land. Grab my guitar and walk behind you down the path, the sun shines and your words make me laugh. 'Cause you're fresh from the shower, got yourself clean and now you tell me how excited you are to get dirty all over again.

Sit beneath our wide brimmed hats, hiding from the sun. Finally got you alone, but the waiting was half the fun. You take off your shades, have to squint to see, and I'm touched that you've done this to share your eyes with me. And I proceed to sing you a love song that wasn't fit for any other man who's come along. I wrote it in a language that makes my heart soar, and you seem to understand, mi amor.

But, oh, how you listen to me, like nothing exists but us and the sea. Undivided attention takes on a whole new meaning, and I feel my heart beating. When I'm finished singing, I must confess, you see, I didn't write that song to sing, I wrote it to be sung to me. You say you had a feeling. I laugh—of course, you do. I don't have to speak, I can just think my words to you.

When you say perhaps you'll sing my song to me, I hold your gaze, and in my eyes I know you see, that would break my heart in the most beautiful way, but perhaps it's been cracked open far enough for one day.

I've waited so long to sing someone that song and have them feel every single word, 'cause when I'm singing my soul, I'm giving my whole self, and it's so very nice to know you heard.

TRAVELING FURTHER OUTWARD

Time expanded.
Clarity showed herself:
Gleaming in the daylight
Shadowed by the sun.

I ran with her.
We were light streaming
Through space and time
Changing colors.

Faster and flying
Within oceans and clouds
Inside the earth
Flowing without limit.

As thought dissolved,
The blurred motion of reality
Stopped.
And left us floating.

We were truth and wonder
Touching all the elements
Of the universe at once.
Traveling further outward.

The end of everything
Met the beginning,
And Clarity dissolved into me
Smiling.

ALL PATHS ARE SPIRALS

There's more beauty here than I can
Express in simple words,
So I undress myself
In a way that peels back my
Version of what is real.

I watch moisture rise
From a freshly rained on surface in the sunshine,
Like the evaporation of conditioning
That has saturated my mind.
I'm sure there's a rainbow arching over me.
Even though I can't see it,
I can still swim in its colors.

I light the first fire of the fall.
There's snow on the mountains.
Most of the leaves are still green,
But they hear the call of change
Sending gold through their veins.

Each breath I take carries within it
The ebb and flow of the tide,
The wax and wane of the moon,
The cycle of seasons beyond thought,
Beyond reason.

For all paths are spirals,
No matter how straight they may appear.

STILL MY MIND

Parallel universe falls through my mind
Like a star in someone else's sky.
Why should I still my chaotic mind
When there's so many directions
My heart wants to fly?

Eyes peer out from the dark of a brim
And roam over my skin.
I step out as who I really am
To face those eyes, and a welcoming grin.

I've been a warrior, and I've been a queen,
Now I find myself somewhere in between.

Singing om shanti, I want to find peace
But I don't want to have to still my mind
And the lover in my heart
Wants to throw her arms around
Every magnificent creature I find.

Stand in the center of my circle
And try to be still,
Bend my will.
Gonna stand in the center of my circle
And try to be still...

ONLY A STORY

It's only a story.
You have to remember…
For good and for glory,
It's only a story.

So let your imagination fly.
Let your imagination fly.

Its beauty sears you alive
And your heart dies a thousand times,
But you grow
With every fight you survive.

For every mountain you climb
You fall farther than you slide,
But you know
In the end you're alive.

I've got angels watching over me. I'm free.
I've got dragons flying over me. I'm free.
I've got faeries watching over me. I'm free.
I've got gods watching over me. I'm free.

'Cause it's only a story.
Try to remember…
For good and for glory,
It's only a story.

So let your imagination fly.
Let your imagination fly.

CREATION AND DESTRUCTION

THEIA, QUEEN OF BRIGHTWOOD, stalked through the shadows in the quietest part of Eldest Grove. Above, evening dimmed to twilight in shades of plum and nightberry, the first stars glittering through openings in the canopy. Twigs and leaves swayed in Theia's hair as she moved in her mysterious way—part dance, part trance, part spell.

She guarded her thoughts, not wanting to infect the forest with her melancholy. Morale was already low. The Weakening had begun to spread across the land, sickening crops and those who ate them. Something drew life force from the collective, and she had yet to discover why.

She'd even sought council with Veska, Queen of the Darkwood, to see if she was behind the Weakening, but she'd said no. Her realm was affected as well.

Wrong as it was, Theia was on the verge of trusting the Dark Queen, which bothered her almost as much as the depletion of life force. She shielded herself, not wanting the trees to know her thoughts. The sorcerer would be furious if he found out.

She'd flirted with Veska, and this wasn't the first time.

She shouldn't dare. Nothing good could come of it. But the Darkwood Queen had walked through Brightwood without hurting a leaf. The danger of her nearness electrified the magic at Theia's core.

Realizing her folly, she'd scared Veska off with requests for rare crystals and legendary jewels. She needed her to think

Theia wasn't worth the trouble. Otherwise, she might confess her love, and the whole affair would be a tragedy for the bards.

Time to remember what was at stake. She had no business dreaming about the Darkwood Queen. She had a duty to the forest. To protect. To nurture. To bring balance.

A story. That would set her right.

Nestled into a nook at the roots of a slumbering tree, Theia sought remembrance of the beginning, before the wholeness was shattered and the fragments estranged. She sighed, growing into the bark at her back, sinking her roots into the soil, seeking the memory in the tree.

There! The record glowed as she caught it in her thought-web and was instantly immersed.

The Sisterhood kept the memories of the earth, passing them down so they knew their past and were ready when the prophecy unfolded. Each forest queen learned how to access the library kept alive in roots and leaves. Many times, it had almost been lost.

This creation story was not the original creation. Still, the memory delivered a nectar-like taste of the completeness that once was. Contentment flooded Theia as she breathed the time of wholeness, when everything thrived in perfect balance. She surrendered to the bliss she knew would be exceedingly brief.

One breath. Two.

Violently bright, a flash from the heavens accompanied a deafening explosion. The ground ripped apart. Theia held onto her tree, knowing it was just a memory but caught in it completely. It shattered her every time.

The earth shook, swallowing entire forests. Trees burned. Some fell into the abyss, others drowned in tidal waves. Worst of all, the pulse of magic seemed to vanish.

Storms ravaged the surviving fragments. Beings that had once co-existed challenged each other in battles that began an unending war.

The trees didn't agree on the cause of the Shattering. Some said the sorcerer cast a spell that went wrong, some said the shock came from the sky. Some said the miners delved too deep, others blamed the dragons.

Maybe an ancient Brightwood queen did something naughty with a Darkwood queen, and they blew up the world.

Stop thinking about dark queens!

Theia brought her consciousness back to the memory, painful as it was. The storms subsided, and the confusion of the trees quieted.

Slowly, magic began to trickle back in. Time blurred as she focused on the ebb and flow of magic. It recovered, but never to what it had been before the Shattering. And now the Weakening threatened it again.

Theia detached from the tree and the memory. She rose, and swayed through the woods, unsatisfied by the story she'd chosen. The life force that sustained them was at risk. She would do whatever was necessary to protect it.

She should find herself a sunshine princess to have a fling with, and squash these romantic thoughts. But a fay voice in the branches of her mind wondered if darkness wasn't part of the key to the prophecy. Did the Weakening signal the beginning of Resurgence? If she welcomed it, would a taste of death kill the magic inside her, or would it ignite rebirth instead?

Night had fallen. Theia didn't need light to find her way out of Eldest Grove. She'd known each tree since she was a sprite. At the edge of the forest, she leaned against a grandmother's trunk, and gazed at the clearing.

Fairies used to play here. A few sparkbugs flitted about, but even the criquits, ribbits and other singers didn't chant their song as loud as they had in the seasons before.

Above, the moon Nessana shone brighter than her siblings, and the stars seemed subdued in comparison. Theia, forest queen, sent a prayer to the moon goddess, determined to find the source of the Weakening by the next full cycle. Even if that meant going to the Darkwood for answers.

Perhaps it was the beginning of the prophecy, as she secretly hoped and feared.

DREAMING

There once was a wish for adventure
That led me to worlds unknown,
And now that I'm on this adventure
I need to choose which way to go.

To ride through the woods to the castle,
Each heartbeat, hoof, and stride.
Then enter the doors and dance 'round the halls,
Riches await inside.

To live in a mountain cabin,
Tend to the hearth and fire,
It's magic I seek with all its mystique,
Revealing my desire.

To sail on the seas in a tall ship,
Feel the wind in the sails wide.
Run my hand o'er the polished wood rail
And watch the dolphins glide.

But none of it has
Quite the appeal
When I see myself there alone.

I'd much prefer
A journey that brings
Us together home.

GATHERING RAINBOWS

Music washes me in color.
Moods of bright rainbows,
Dark storm clouds,
Solitary stars,
And the soft, mysterious
Gradients of dawn and dusk.

Songs are tapestries of sound
Woven with resonance and feeling.
Poetry in layers of harmony.

Music takes the ordeals of humanity
And instills transformation,
Morphing suffering into sanctuary.

Songs paint pictures that
Take flight and come to life.

SUNBEAMS

Dance on sunbeams.
Talk to the trees and kiss the wind.
Let the ocean be your intuition,
Let the mountains be your strength.

Feel the earth breathe.

Listen.
Learn.
Wonder.

Understand.

SLEEPING ON DRAGON'S WINGS

Eyes heavy, breath slow,
I surrender to the pull.
Sleep's irresistible tide
Takes me under.

I fall into fathomless night,
Wind in my hair.
Wings beat a breathy bass drum.
whoomp, whoomp, whoomp

He dives beneath and catches me.
Dragon of my heart,
Friend of my soul,
Carrying me onward.

Scales like stars, he flies,
The sky of dreams is ours.
Rest, he whispers.
I will take you home.

STARDUST AND HEARTWOOD

STAR WHITE ON BLACK CANVAS, a goddess sparks into being. She dances, making fractals of herself, sprinkling stardust down through the night.

On earth, the trees shiver. Magic rains on their leaves, and they awaken, tree spirits cloaked in flesh. They dance, as they always do when granted this rare gift. They know it will fade with the dawn.

One dryad runs wide through the forest, away from her cedar self. Arms spread, back arched, she spins, hair like starlight. Delighting in the thrill of embodiment.

A hunter watches. This is not the stag he seeks. This is a beauty so rare he should look away. But he can't. She is luminous, every dizzying step taken in irresistible, feral grace. He leaves his weapons, and when she twirls towards his shadow, he steps into the dance.

He is a mortal. She is the illusion of immortality.

Entranced, they do not speak. They spiral in the darkness to a song whispered through branch and root and heartwood. Its rhythm drives them on with glorious power.

When they reach the river, they stop, drinking in breaths of mist. And though she knows it will be her doom, the dryad walks with the hunter towards the dawn.

"What is your name?" His hand is strong. Warm. He has blood beneath his flesh, while she has starlight and sap.

"Stellia." She should run. Should never have danced with him. But she cannot pull away now. Her heart flies like a hummingbird.

"I am Wolfe." Perhaps he looks like one. A little. His hair is wild, but the dance did that.

Her hair streams down her back and glimmers in the darkness. He sees it. Touches it.

"What are you?" His voice is barely a whisper. He stops walking, eyes aglow in the shimmer of her skin.

"I am the goddess at play." It is a truth. There are many truths. Some she cannot tell.

He takes her as he did in the dance, one hand low on her back, the other capturing hers. He brings it to his mouth. His beard is rough but his lips are soft as they brush against her fingers.

Stellia closes her eyes. When she opens them, his face is a hand's breadth away. She sways, missing her roots, sure she will fall, but he doesn't let her. He pulls her closer. His kiss is kinder than a morning breeze, more quenching than an afternoon rain. It warms her like summer sunshine though the night is cool.

She trembles as if caught in a storm, but willingly. She would face the fall of her tree, risk being engulfed in flame if it would mean she could stay in this embrace of magic as powerful as the one who made her.

But that chance is not on offer.

Dawn marches steadily towards them. She wants to tell him. One dance is all she gets. Sometimes the goddess doesn't wake her again for years.

Knowing she must return to her tree before the sun touches her leaves or she will burn into nothing, she puts her fingers on his lips. Takes a small step back.

His eyes darken, need and awe and something more in their depths. He follows when she turns, moving towards her grove, twisting the winding path they'd danced, her hand in his the whole way.

She doesn't stop until her canopy encloses them, branches dropping low like arms of secrecy. Her tree. Her home. Only here does she turn to face him again.

"Stellia." He caresses her face. Her name is spoken like a prayer.

She should tell him, but she can't bear to waste a moment in heartbreak, even if part of her already mourns. There will be time for grief after the sun dissolves the enchantment.

With her heartwood behind him, her chest pressed to his, she leans in to taste his kiss. He responds with such force, stirs with such passion, she's convinced there's a star burning within him.

This is a different kind of dance. Touch and breath, wrapped around each other, they blaze together in the shadows of her tree. She soars, though they lie on soft moss between her roots. Her leaves inhale his every breath. Her dryad skin drinks his sweat like dew.

His kisses are hungry, then tender, then all consuming. His strength surrounds her, but his gaze is pure vulnerability. She would give him her spark to make this live on.

In the desperate dregs of fleeting night, she offers her surrender.

This is my stardust soul, she whispers in her heart. *And it is yours.*

Star bright and golden, the goddess rises with the dawn to see what has become of her temporal tree spirits. Most have danced until their heartwood called them home, but one dances still.

And she has found a mortal. A hunter, no less.

They make love beneath her branches, their passion so great it outshines the creeping sun. Still, it cannot save them. The goddess could intervene, but mortal lives are short, and the night is already over.

Yet the magic has taken on a life of its own. And the stardust, in its fading glory, does a thing both beautiful and terrible. When dawn comes to claim her, the soul of Stellia splits. A seed abandons its home to live within her lover.

She doesn't scream, though her tree will bear the scar until it rots. The goddess can taste Stellia's tears like bittersweet wine made of honeyed betrayal, and she savors the possibilities, acting on none.

She has his seed, he has hers. That is balance enough.

The dryad retreats to her trunk. Dawn smudges the sky with rose-blood light.

The hunter gasps as Stellia fades, her image melting into the tree, their hands touching until there is only bark. When the sun shines, warm and golden on the man, he burns a little. But the stardust within him doesn't die.

He kisses the tree.

Once.

Gently.

And weeps as he walks away.

FROM THE KEEPER

WORDS ON PAGES don't capture the fullness of Shelta's gift. They're only a taste of her music.

A hint of her magic.

Shelta doesn't know how powerful she is, nor how her songs bind the worlds. One day, she'll understand. My unspoken hope is that she finds her way to the Realm of the Gods, where we can help her. Train her. Perhaps, I can entice her to give me a private concert.

For now, I'll watch from the stars as she finds her way, and listen in rapture as her music weaves threads through the tapestry, collecting songs and stories in her wake.

If you enjoyed this book, please leave a review!

One of the nicest things you can do for an author is leave a review. Reviews can be posted wherever you purchased this book, at Goodreads.com and Bookbub.com, and shared on social media if you have friends who might enjoy the read.

Sign up for Leia Talon's newsletter to get the latest on book releases: www.LeiaTalon.com/newsletter

Read on for the beginning of

The first novel in the *Roots and Stars* series,
where Shelta finds her way home.

FALLING THROUGH THE WEAVING

CHAPTER 1

The Relentless Squeeze of Time

THERE WAS NO ESCAPING the bite of regret. Not when I was saying goodbye to a setup as nice as this—digs near the beach, walking distance from prime busking territory, and a pair of friends I didn't want to leave. I squinted at the distant ocean glittering in the sun as I took in the view one last time, a salty breeze drifting through the window.

With a sharp-edged blossom of sorrow in my belly, I stroked the blonde wood of my guitar, scuffed from years of playing music on the street. Stevie loved this six-string. Now it would be his. It was cowardly, not waiting for him and Jess to come home before taking off, but I sucked at saying goodbye. The note tucked between the strings was the best I could do.

Sweet Jess & Stevie,

I can't explain why, but it's time for me to move on. Enjoy the guitar. Remember me with laughter and kisses and songs. I adore you both. ~ Shelta

Anchor-heavy heart sinking in my chest, I adjusted my leggings and skirt. Grabbed my coat and backpack. Out the door I went, without a backward glance. Down the stairs. Onto the street.

The Pacific Ocean crashed on the beach not far from Jess and Stevie's apartment on Vancouver Island. One of the nicer spots I'd lived. Stevie had brought me home; Jess had decided to keep me. We'd had such fun, us three: jamming for tips on Government Street, waxing poetic over bottles of wine, getting tangled up in one another. I'd never see them again. Like so many others I'd left behind.

I had no roots. I'd fast-forwarded through eight decades in my thirty-odd years. At this point, I'd try anything to stop the pull of time. I hoped the shimmering red dragon that kept showing up in my dreams held the key. Its message last night made me pack up this morning.

Come. Find me. It's time.

I couldn't get him out of my mind. He was different than the others that frequented my dreams—small ones who curled up with me when I was lonely or cold, big ones who flew with power that made my soul soar even when I was at my lowest in my waking hours. I'd seen the crimson dragon before, but only from afar. Lately, he was all I dreamt about.

The ocean breeze was no match for the merciless heat of the sun. It beat against the buildings and radiated up from the sidewalks. I didn't let it slow my stride. I had a purpose. A problem. Somehow, I had to escape the vicious cycle that stole everyone I'd ever loved.

Sweat dampened my calves. The tall boots were overkill, but it would be cooler in the forest, and who knew what season it would be wherever I landed. My long, dark-green coat flapped as I walked, and my fingers rubbed the wine-red embroidery at the cuffs in a habitual motion. The coat's weight was a comfort. I'd slept in it more nights than I liked to admit and had managed to hang onto it for three time jumps. Only my dragon necklace had been with me longer.

It didn't take long to reach the highway out of town, and I stationed myself along the widest part of the road, hoping to hitch a ride. Cars and trucks flew past, hot air and exhaust buffeting me in their wake. I didn't always stick my thumb out. I took a chance on the vehicles that looked friendly, trusting a gut feeling I'd learned to listen to back in my twenties, when I'd done more hitchhiking than was wise in an attempt to outrun fate—and failed miserably.

Sweat was trickling down the back of my neck by the time a weathered woman in a dented pick-up gave me a lift. Friendly sort. Talker. She told me her thoughts on the latest horrors done by the usual regimes determined to rule the world. People were disappearing. Murderers walked free, protected by their uniforms. Atrocities I could do nothing about.

Numb, I only half-listened.

She dropped me off at the edge of a forest that stretched halfway across the island, then pulled away with a cloud of dust. I ventured into the woods. The cool shadows were a godsend as I followed a trail north, toward the bigger trees.

Ferns swatted at my thighs. Leaves and moss cushioned my footsteps. The bright blue sky seemed to mock my apprehension, towering trees dimming the too-cheerful light.

Foreboding clouds would've been more fitting for my mood.

After almost an hour, I ducked off the path and cut through the bush on a thin wildlife trail, letting my intuition guide me. On I marched, feet keeping time with the music in my head and the dragon's echoing words.

Come. Find me. It's time.

I caught myself hoping, dreaming that wherever the wormhole took me, it would be an improvement. Foolhardy optimism. Civilization was messy no matter the year. 2035 had been no different. Yes, I'd found friends. Things had worked out for me. Always did. I could never understand why.

But the state of the world? It didn't get better. My struggles were nothing compared to what so many people faced. Animals, too. It was devastating. Anxiety came clawing every time I dwelled on how helpless I was to do anything about it.

I pushed the air out of my lungs. Inhaled.

Calm, Shelta. Focus.

My heart beat its relentless boom, making a drum out of my chest. Douglas fir and cedar grew all around, the air scented with golden sap and sun-warmed trees. Their thick trunks and tapering heights reminded me of ancient sentries. When a massive fir caught my eye, I trudged through the underbrush toward it, over logs half-decomposed on the forest floor. A knot of expectation formed in my belly as I reached out to touch the rough, reddish bark.

Nothing happened. This wasn't the right tree.

Disappointment sparked cynical thoughts as I returned to the deer path I'd been following. It was always a tree, every unasked-for jump—except maybe when I was born. Mother-Number-One swore I'd come from "the belly of the goddess." Whatever that meant. But I'd never been able to make the time leap happen myself. Every time I'd intentionally sought the tree, it had eluded me. Then when I least expected it, a mere brush against the wrong branch would suck me forward a few years and plop me down in a new forest. A new city or village. A new library full of books that didn't have the answers I was looking for.

Seventeen time leaps in my thirty-odd years. I'd had nine foster mothers along the way. Countless friends and lovers who'd taken me in. The memories eventually blended into music. Sometimes I forgot the people on purpose, and just remembered the songs.

The dragon's call might've simply been my subconscious urging me to move on, but what if it was a premonition? Maybe there was an actual dragon waiting for me somewhere. Somehow, I'd find a way to control the damn time travel.

If I was going to keep being dragged into the future, I wanted some say in the details of my departure. I wasn't leaving this forest until I found the right tree. It was the only move I had in a game I didn't understand.

From the place in my soul where the music came from, a pull drove me deeper into the woods. I reached for the dragon pendant at my neck, tracing the small circle of body, wings and tail, the one silver eye on its curled head a familiar notch beneath my fingertips.

A song welled up at a turn in the terrain, and I opened my mouth to set the wordless melody free. The flow of notes came without thought, full of promise and mystery. Hope, even.

My feet seemed to float, each stride pulling me forward, until I rounded the roots of a downed giant and crossed a small clearing to a massive cedar. It towered above me, emitting a subtle glow that pulsed and bled one color into another. Blue. Purple. Gold. Green.

I stopped in my tracks, silence stealing my song. The humid air tasted electric. Charged. Thick with potency and power.

Found the tree.

The portal's presence was intimidating, to the point that I almost wanted to turn back. None of the trees I'd gone through before had *glowed.* But I didn't want to repeat the same pattern I'd been helpless to my whole life. This was different. Good.

In a desperate rush of optimism, I envisioned my version of utopia: a peaceful world where people respected each other and the earth. Twenty years into the future, maybe? However long it took for humanity to figure out that waging war and destroying the planet were awful ideas, that's when I wanted to land.

I sucked in a shaky breath. Forced myself forward. Reached both hands through the pulsing, translucent light to the soft-bark trunk of the tree. The second I touched it, everything went rainbow-black and all the music in creation streamed through my head at once in a seasick symphony. The world dropped away.

Falling.

Falling.

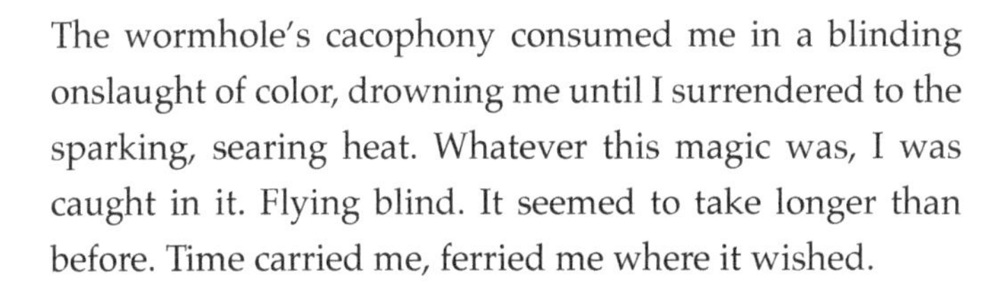

The wormhole's cacophony consumed me in a blinding onslaught of color, drowning me until I surrendered to the sparking, searing heat. Whatever this magic was, I was caught in it. Flying blind. It seemed to take longer than before. Time carried me, ferried me where it wished.

And spat me out through a wall of startling silence, into the next place.

The ground heaved like a ship's deck. Head spinning, both hands up, I staggered to my feet and blinked through blurry vision at the sight of a shaggy-haired man on his knees at the edge of a clear pool. His head was bowed, as if in prayer. I could've sworn the image of a red-haired woman glowed in his reflection, but it was gone with a swirl of water.

Seeing me, the man sprang to his feet, sword in hand and legs tense beneath a dark green kilt. Behind him, a horse pawed the ground. I braced myself to keep from toppling over, and squeezed my eyes shut to clear my head. Slowly, reality came into focus, and I tried to get my bearings. Clouds lurked above a sparse canopy of trees, and a brisk wind raked leaves from the branches of a giant oak beside me.

The man lowered his sword and opened his mouth with a throaty sound that wasn't quite a word. "Are ye all right?" he finally asked.

I tried a smile, failed, and then tried again with more success. "I will be."

"Where did ye come from, lass?"

Scotland. I was in Scotland. But unless swords were back in fashion, something had gone terribly wrong. Backwards in time didn't appeal to me in the least. I'd only ever gone forward before. My mind stuttered. I put my hands to my head and suppressed a groan, glad the pool of water separated us for the time being. I had no idea how to explain myself.

Attempting to regain cognitive ability gave me a chance to look him over. Solid build. Sharp gaze.

Unmistakably wearing a kilt. His boots were taller than mine, with buckles up the sides, their leather not quite as black as his coat. Black, blue, and white stripes crossed the forest green of his plaid, and a sword hung at his left hip, mirrored by a dagger on his right. A scar on his left temple peeked out from bits of dark hair that fell to his jaw, where another scar shot a streak of silver through a rough beard.

"Ye appeared out of thin air a moment ago." He tried again. "Singing, if I'm not mistaken."

"Singing. Yeah, I tend to do that." My gaze dropped to the flow of water between us as circuits connected in my brain. "I was walking through a forest in Canada. There was a really big tree. I touched it, and now I'm here." I didn't know what else to say, considering he'd seen me materialize. I'd never had witnesses before.

"Ye travel between worlds?" His voice was little more than a whisper.

I lifted my eyes. "I guess so." Would he think me a witch?

He stayed silent, but I didn't pick up any sense of alarm, so I summoned my courage and asked an absurd question that needed sorting in order for my brain to deal. "Am I correct in thinking I'm in Scotland?"

"Aye. Ye're a long way from the New World, if that is indeed where ye came from."

"British Columbia."

"Never heard of it."

"Oh." It was a small sound. Distant. "I'm sorry I interrupted whatever you were doing here." My apology floated slack over the water. How far back had I gone? I turned around to touch the tree, the oak's bark bumpy while the cedar's had been smooth, but the portal was closed. Like always. There was no way out. I forced my gaze back to the man across the spring.

"Ye haven't interrupted." His words were as lacking in conviction as mine.

I *had* interrupted something. I knew it with the same certainty that warned me I was an outrageously long way from anything familiar. "Would you be so kind as to tell me the year?"

"1753," he replied evenly. "What year was it where ye came from?"

"2035," I whispered.

His eyebrows shot up. Was that fear in his gaze? I needed him to trust me or my odds of survival would drop fast.

"I know it's hard to believe." I lifted my fingers to trace the dragon on my necklace.

He narrowed his eyes when he saw the pendant, something like recognition in the crinkle of his face. "Aye. That's a mighty long jump."

Shelta's story continues in

ACKNOWLEDGEMENTS

This book wouldn't have been possible without the support of my family, especially my parents. Thank you for providing every opportunity for me to grow, and for nurturing my creativity all my life.

Big gratitude to Phil Sheaff for giving me my first guitar and climbing hills and mountains with me so I could sing into the sky.

Special thanks to Rebecca Fryar, John King, Samantha Nimmo, Belinda Grant, and D. Lambert for your valuable feedback. Beth W. Patterson, Elysia Lumen Strife, Kat Turner, Avery Ames, Alex Forbes, and everyone who reviewed an ARC, you are so appreciated. To Tara Findlay, Jena Skai, Dawn Denise and Benjamin Ward, Suniva Bronson, Sue O'Shaughnessy, Rhonda Kay, Saffisara, Witty, Snook, the Ninja Sharks and PitSquirrels—everyone who has believed in me, your names are too many to list, but your encouragement means the world!

This book is dedicated to Robert Ramos, who named me Hokule'a and taught me how to surf. Your love of the ocean and music were an inspiration. I hope the seas of Heaven give you perfect, endless waves. Your kindness lives in my heart, and your joy shines in the stars.

Leia Talon writes fantasy and speculative fiction with romantic elements. Her lyrical approach is influenced by a lifetime of turning emotions into poetry and songs.

Shelta's Songbook opens the universe of the *World Tree Chronicles,* paving the way for two series of novels: *Roots and Stars* and *Dragons and Gods*.

Follow Leia's blog for favorite reads and insights on writing life, and sign up for her newsletter to get the latest on upcoming books.

www.LeiaTalon.com

Twitter/Facebook/Instagram: @LeiaTalon

CPSIA information can be obtained
at www.ICGtesting.com
Printed in the USA
BVHW071632181220
595733BV00002B/212

9 780987 992338